W9-BIH-533

Mindy Kim and the
Fairy-Tale Wedding

**Don't miss more fun adventures
with Mindy Kim!**

Mindy Kim

and the
Fairy-Tale
Wedding

BOOK
7

By Lyla Lee
Illustrated by Dung Ho

ALADDIN
New York London Toronto Sydney New Delhi

This book is a work of fiction. Any references to historical events, real people, or real places are used fictitiously. Other names, characters, places, and events are products of the author's imagination, and any resemblance to actual events or places or persons, living or dead, is entirely coincidental.

🦋 ALADDIN
An imprint of Simon & Schuster Children's Publishing Division
1230 Avenue of the Americas, New York, New York 10020
First Aladdin hardcover edition April 2022
Text copyright © 2022 by Lyla Lee
Illustrations copyright © 2022 by Dung Ho
Also available in an Aladdin paperback edition.
All rights reserved, including the right of reproduction in whole or in part in any form.
ALADDIN and related logo are registered trademarks of Simon & Schuster, Inc.
For information about special discounts for bulk purchases, please contact Simon & Schuster Special Sales at 1-866-506-1949 or business@simonandschuster.com.
The Simon & Schuster Speakers Bureau can bring authors to your live event. For more information or to book an event contact the Simon & Schuster Speakers Bureau at 1-866-248-3049 or visit our website at www.simonspeakers.com.
Designed by Laura Lyn DiSiena
The illustrations for this book were rendered digitally.
The text of this book was set in Haboro.
Manufactured in the United States of America 0222 FFG
10 9 8 7 6 5 4 3 2 1
Library of Congress Control Number 2021940847
ISBN 978-1-5344-8901-1 (hc)
ISBN 978-1-5344-8900-4 (pbk)
ISBN 978-1-5344-8902-8 (ebook)

For my parents, whose wedding video inspired this book

Chapter 1

My name is Mindy Kim. I am nine years old. And I am so excited for this weekend. My dad is getting married!

Since I've never been to a wedding before, I don't know what to expect. But my best friend, Sally, says that weddings are pretty and fun. So I am very excited!

"My cousin got married in Hawaii!" Sally told me. "It was at the beach, and sand got everywhere, but it was worth it. It was the perfect fairy-tale wedding!"

Dad isn't getting married in Hawaii, but I hope

his wedding is going to be a perfect fairy-tale wedding too. He and his fiancée, Julie, deserve the best day ever!

At the end of the school day on Thursday, Dad picked me up from school. Usually, my babysitter, Eunice, picks me up, but today was a special day. We were going to get our relatives from the airport! My grandparents, uncle, aunt, and cousins were all coming from Korea for Dad and Julie's special day.

When I got into Dad's car, he looked super nervous. He was holding the steering wheel so hard, his knuckles were white!

"Appa, are you okay?" I asked him as we left the carpool lane. *Appa* is the Korean word for "Daddy." I call him Appa or Dad, because they mean the same thing.

"Huh? Oh, I'm fine, Mindy. Everything just feels very real now that our family's coming all the way here from Korea. And Julie's family is coming from New York and China."

The only people to ever visit us in America were my grandparents, and they only visited while we lived in California. This was the first time anyone in my family was coming to see us in Florida. I hoped they'd like it here as much as I do!

"I can't wait to see everyone!" I said. "Do you think they'll bring Danbi?"

Danbi the Pomeranian is my cousins' dog. She isn't as sweet and nice as my dog, Theodore the Mutt, but she's still really adorable!

At a stoplight, Dad glanced over to smile at me. "Probably not. Sorry, honey. Remember how we couldn't bring Theodore with us to Korea? They're coming for the wedding, and then only spending another week traveling around the US after that. It's too short a trip for dogs!"

I was a little disappointed, but it was okay. Even though they weren't bringing their dog, I was so happy that I could see my family again!

I checked the back seat to make sure that Dad

had brought my sign. When I visited my family in Korea, they made me a sign to welcome me at the airport! I wanted to return the favor by making a sign of my own.

It had Danbi's face on it, so it was kind of awkward now that I knew she wasn't coming. But at least the sign was still cute! I used bright and eye-catching colors like pink and yellow and sprinkled lots of glitter on it. I hoped my family would be able to see my sign from miles and miles away!

Dad still looked anxious, so I told him, "Don't be nervous, Appa. Everyone's coming to see you and Julie! The wedding will go great! I just know it!"

He smiled. "Thanks, Mindy. You're right. I should think more positively, even though we still have a lot of work to do before the wedding on Sunday."

And then we got on the highway. Orlando International Airport, here we come!

Chapter 2

At the airport, Dad and I waited at the arrivals area for our relatives to come out. The airport was busy, as usual, with people going in and out of the terminals. It reminded me of how *they* waited for *us* when we went to Korea in the summer!

I held my sign up high and waved it around. A few people looked our way as they passed and smiled.

Thankfully, we didn't have to wait long before my family came out. And just like I hoped they would, they spotted my sign and waved at us right away!

My uncle and grandpa were pushing carts

loaded with lots of suitcases. Dad rushed forward to help Grandpa with his cart.

My cousins, Sung-jin and Sora, looked wide awake and really excited, but everyone else looked tired. Grandma and Grandpa especially looked exhausted!

"Min-jung!" Grandma said, pulling me into a big hug. "It's so good to see you!"

Min-jung is my Korean name. I like both Mindy and Min-jung, but my relatives usually just call me by my Korean name. It makes sense, because we talk to one another in Korean!

In Grandma's arms, I breathed in deep. She still smelled like steamed buns and other yummy foods. Back in Korea, she made us so many different things that I thought that my belly was going to explode! Her cooking is the best in the entire universe.

"Hi, Halmeoni!" I said, using the Korean word for Grandma. "I'm so glad you're here! How was your flight?"

"My knees are aching from sitting too long, but it was still good!" she replied. "I think I'm getting too old for flying, though."

"Yes, it was a good flight, but still very tiring," Grandpa agreed.

"That's okay," I said. "We'll just have to visit you in Korea next time!"

I had no problems with that. Korea was so fun, and I learned so much about my culture the last time we went. I can't wait to go there again!

"You're always welcome in our apartment, Min-jung!" my uncle said.

"Thanks, Keun Appa!" I said.

In Korea, people use different words for uncles or aunts, depending on how they're related to your parents! Since this uncle is Dad's big brother, I call him Keun Appa and call his wife Keun Umma.

"Grandma and I have a gift for you!" Grandpa said.

He pulled out a teddy bear from behind his back. But it wasn't just a regular teddy bear. It was a teddy bear dressed in a pink hanbok! A hanbok is traditional Korean clothing. It looked so cute and funny on the bear!

"Your harabeoji saw it at the airport and said he just had to buy it for you," Keun Appa said with a laugh.

"It's a very good gift!" Dad said.

"Yeah! Thanks, Harabeoji! I love it. It's so adorable!"

Grandpa smiled. "No problem. I'm glad you like it."

While we were walking to the airport parking lot, Sora, my baby cousin, tugged at my shirt. "Is your home close to the airport? Let's go! I'm hungry."

Everyone laughed. Sora is three years younger than me, and she is really cute.

"It's an hour and thirty minutes away," I said. "But we'll get there in no time!"

Both Sora and Sung-jin, my older cousin, gasped.

"That's so far!" Sung-jin said. "In Korea, if
go that far, you're not even in the same state!"

"In America, it's not that bad," Dad explaine
"I think Florida alone is almost twice as big as
South Korea."

"Wow," exclaimed Sung-jin. "America really is big!"

While Dad took half the bags to our car, Keun
Appa took the other half and went to rent a van.
Dad's car is plenty big for driving around Dad,
Julie, and me, but it doesn't have enough seats for
six other people.

My cousins and I went in Dad's car, while my
grandparents rode in Keun Appa's. As we drove
back to our house, Sora and Sung-jin stared out
the windows.

"Florida is so pretty!" Sora said. "The palm trees
are so tall!"

"Wait until you see the beach!" I said. I was
really glad that my cousins thought Florida was
beautiful too!

When we got home, Theodore the Mutt came running to the door to greet my relatives. Everyone petted him and said he was very cute. I was so happy that my family finally got a chance to meet Theodore!

"Danbi would love him!" Sora said. "I bet they'd be instant friends."

At that moment, she frowned a little, like she missed her dog. I could relate, since that's how I'd felt when we left Theodore to go to Korea.

"I think they'd be friends too," I replied, trying to cheer her up. "Hopefully, they can meet someday!"

Soon afterward, Julie arrived at our house with her family. Her parents and sisters had flown in from China and New York the night before.

It was my first time meeting Julie's family. Her mom's smile was the same as Julie's, while her dad's kind eyes looked like hers. One of Julie's sisters had the same smile, while the other had the same eyes

We all went around to say hi to one anoth

When it was time for me to greet Julie's par

Julie's mom said, "And you must be Mindy! You're even more adorable in person than you look in the pictures Julie sent us! Here, Julie said you liked animals, so we got you this! Cats are good luck in Chinese culture."

She gave me a key chain with a small stuffed-animal cat. It was so cute!

Afterward, we ate dinner. Dad had bought a lot of yummy foods from the Korean market. While we were eating, we talked about our plans. Our dinner table was more crowded than I'd ever seen it, but the smiling faces and laughter made me feel warm and fuzzy inside. We were all one big happy family!

Dad, Julie, and their parents spent most of dinner talking about the wedding preparations. It sounded like we were going to be busy for the rest of the week! Tomorrow, Julie's sisters had to make some last-minute preparations for the wedding too, so my aunt and uncle were going to take us kids around town.

"Mindy, it's going to be your job to show everyone around!" Dad said. "But remember to have lots of fun in the meantime."

"Sure thing!" I said. I was glad I could help out in some way.

Soon it was time for bed. Julie and her family went back to her house, while Dad and I got things ready for our family at ours. Since our house doesn't have enough beds for everyone, we laid out a thick blanket in the living room so my cousins, aunt, and uncle could sleep there while Grandma and Grandpa took the guest bedroom. No one seemed to mind. In Korea, lots of people sleep on the floor.

That night, I was so excited to show everyone around that I had a hard time sleeping. I hoped my family would like our neighborhood as much as I did!

Chapter 3

The next day was Friday, but I didn't go to school. Not only did I have plans to hang out with all my cousins, but it was also the start of the wedding weekend! So Dad let me take the day off.

Dad and Julie were both going to work today. Dad explained that they didn't want to take the day off because they had to take lots of time off for their honeymoon trip.

"I'll be back home early so we can all go to the wedding rehearsal later," he said as he left. "Have fun with everyone, Mindy!"

"Okay, Appa! Have a good day at work!"

After breakfast, Keun Umma asked, "What do you guys want to do today?"

Sora perked up. "Beach! Let's go to the beach!"

"Yeah!" said Sung-jin.

"The beach is only twenty minutes away from our house," I said. "It's right by my school. We can go there!"

"Okay, sounds good!" Keun Appa said. "Be sure to put on lots of sunscreen. We'll leave when everyone's ready!"

"Yay!" my cousins and I cheered.

We changed into our swimsuits and put on lots of sunscreen. My swimsuit was sky blue and had a pink dolphin on it. Dolphins are my favorite sea animals!

Keun Appa also changed into his swim trunks, but Keun Umma and my grandparents just put on comfortable clothes.

"We're still a little too tired from the flight to play in the water," Grandpa explained. "You kids should still have fun! We'll be walking along the shore."

Before we left, I went to Dad's bathroom to get towels for the entire family. And then we were beach ready!

When we arrived, my relatives' jaws dropped open at the beach's white sand and blue-green water.

"Wow!" Sora said. "It's so pretty!"

"Yeah!" Sung-jin said. "The water looks so different from the water at the beach in Korea!"

"That's probably because the Pacific Ocean is around Korea, while this is the Atlantic!" Keun Appa explained. "The water is warmer, which makes it look different."

"I hope we get to see turtles," Sung-jin said. "I heard there are a lot of turtles in Florida. And sharks!"

Sora and I gulped.

"I've never seen a shark in the water before," I said. "So hopefully it's safe!"

"We'll just have to be careful," Keun Appa said. "And only go to the shallow water!"

As soon as the car stopped, my cousins and I got out and ran to the shore.

"Don't forget to take off your shoes before you get in the water!" said Keun Umma. "And watch out for jellyfish!"

Keun Appa caught up and splashed around in the water with us. Everyone laughed, and we all had a good time. It was so fun to be able to play with my family!

After, we lay out on the beach towels by the shore and talked about the big day.

"Are you excited for the wedding, Min-jung?" asked Grandpa. "And for Julie to officially join your family?"

"Yup!" I said. "I've never been to a wedding before, but I hope it'll be *beautiful*! And once everything is over, it'll be so nice to have another girl in the house. Sometimes, between Dad and Theodore, I feel outnumbered!"

Everyone laughed.

"Julie's really fun and nice. She loves Dad and me, and we love her right back! It'll be fun for us to all live in the same house together! And we won't have to stop to pick her up from her house whenever we go on adventures."

"I bet you can't wait to eat Julie's cooking every day," Grandma said with a wink.

I gave her a wide grin.

"She's not as good as you, Halmeoni. And Dad's not bad either. But Julie is definitely a better cook than him!"

"Julie is fantastic!" Keun Umma said. "The food she made when you all were visiting was very delicious."

"Speaking of food, I think that's enough beach time for today," Keun Appa said. "And I don't know about you, but I'm getting hungry! Do you have any good lunch recommendations, Min-jung?"

"Yeah! I know a good pizza place!" I exclaimed. "Dad and I go there every month. We won free pizza from a competition at the school!" I smiled, remembering how fun it was to be on that trivia team with Dad, Julie, and Sally and her family!

"Yay!" Sora cheered. "I love pizza!"

"Same here!" said Sung-jin.

We piled into the car and drove over to Signor Morelli's. Because Dad and I had been there so many times, I knew exactly what we should get: a stuffed-crust double-pepperoni pizza!

It was my relatives' first time eating American pizza, and everyone loved it!

"The crust isn't as good as the sweet-potato crust we have back home, but it's definitely bigger, and still really yummy!" said Sung-jin.

"Sweet-potato crust?" I exclaimed. "That sounds amazing!"

The next time we were in Korea, I was definitely going to ask Dad to take me to a Korean pizza place!

As we all ate, I told my cousins about my life

here in Florida, while they told me about their life in Korea.

"Here we only go to school five days a week," I explained. "Monday through Friday!"

Sung-jin groaned. "That's so lucky! In Korea, we don't have to go to school on Saturday, but I still have tutoring and other classes. And then I have taekwondo and piano practice after."

It felt weird but also nice to eat lunch with my family. It reminded me of what Sally said once about what it's like to eat dinner with her sisters. I don't have siblings, but I imagined this was what it must feel like to have them.

The pizza tasted a thousand times better than usual with everyone happily eating with me at the table. I wished my cousins lived closer to us so we could have meals like this all the time!

Chapter 4

After we got back from Signor Morelli's, I played video games with my cousins until it was time for the wedding rehearsal. It felt weird to not be at school on a Friday, but it was also fun. I wished I could always have no school on Fridays!

When Dad got back from work, we all changed into nice clothes for the rehearsal.

I put on a blue dress with pink flowers and a poofy skirt. Even though tonight was just practice, I still wanted to wear something with flowers, since I was the flower girl!

On our way out the door, I scooped Theodore

the Mutt into my arms. He's a very important member of our family, so I wanted him to be part of the ceremony. I was training him to be the ring bearer!

The wedding was going to be at a nice hotel by the beach. We met up with Julie and her family and went to the back of the hotel. The ceremony was going to be outdoors, on a deck overlooking the ocean.

People stared at Theodore as we walked by, but I hugged him tight. Dad and Julie didn't say anything about Theodore, so I was sure it was okay!

When we went out onto the hotel's deck, everyone gasped. The sun was setting, and the view of the ocean from where we were standing was so beautiful! Seagulls flew above our heads, and the water looked extra sparkly from the golden sunlight.

Dad pulled Julie into a quick hug. They looked so happy!

Everyone got in their places for the rehearsal.

When it was almost my turn to go down the aisle, I put Theodore down so I could grab my flower-girl basket from one of the chairs. He started walking around while sniffing the deck. He looked really excited!

"Wait!" Dad cried out. "Mindy, you brought Theodore here?"

Uh-oh.

Everyone stared at Theodore and me.

I bit my lip. "Yeah! He's going to be the ring bearer! You didn't say anything, so I thought it was okay."

Dad groaned. "I must have been too busy getting ready to notice. Mindy, I know Theodore is a member of this family, but weddings aren't the best place for dogs."

"Theodore can behave!" I said. "I promise! I trained him a lot, especially for the big day."

Dad glanced at Julie, who looked worried.

She and Dad whispered back and forth before Dad said, "Okay, Mindy. He can stay. I'm sure you worked really hard to train him!"

I didn't have real flower petals like I would at the

real wedding, but I still pretended to throw flower petals on the deck as Julie walked behind me. It was fun at first, but then I started thinking about how everyone at the wedding would be watching me. And *then* I thought about how mad and scared Dad looked when he noticed Theodore. Eunice and I had worked hard to train Theodore for the wedding. I thought Dad was going to love the surprise, not hate it!

My heart beat really fast, and I felt queasy.

Then something terrible happened. I tripped!

"Oh no!" I cried out. My basket went flying backward out of my hand and almost hit Julie in the head. Everyone gasped. Julie ducked out of the way. It crashed onto the deck, scaring Theodore!

Before I could stop him, Theodore went off running around in circles and barking loudly.

Everyone covered their ears. Dad and Julie looked horrified.

"Shh, Theodore!" I hissed, trying to calm him

down. "Shhh, quiet down, buddy—it's okay!"

I tried to catch him, but he slipped out of my grasp and ran off the deck and out onto the beach. This was a big disaster!

"Bad dog!" I yelled. "Come back here!"

I went running after Theodore, and so did my cousins. By the time we caught him, our clothes were soaking wet from the waves and covered in sand.

Oh no. Dad and Julie weren't going to be happy about this.

When we came back onto the deck, Dad said, "Mindy, maybe you and Theodore should sit the rest of the evening out. We don't have much rehearsal time left."

Everyone was frowning at me. I stared down at my feet as I picked up Theodore and went to go sit down on a nearby bench. I felt bad. I didn't want to ruin the wedding! But I also hoped that this didn't mean that Theodore and I couldn't participate in the real thing.

When rehearsal was over, I apologized to Dad and Julie.

"I'm sorry, and Theodore is sorry too!" I said. "See?"

We all looked down at Theodore, who gave a little whimper and lay down with his head on his paws.

Even though dogs can't talk, he sure looked really embarrassed!

"I'll be more careful at the wedding, so I won't trip and scare Theodore again," I continued. "He's usually a really good ring bearer, I promise! Please let us be part of the real thing?"

Dad gave me a big hug, and Julie joined in.

"Of course you can participate in the wedding, Mindy!" Dad replied. "You're our MVP! But Theodore . . . I really don't think he should come to the wedding. It was a mistake to bring him today, and I'm sorry I was too busy getting ready to tell you that before we left."

My shoulders drooped. Just thinking about Theodore being home alone during this important family event made me sad.

But then I got an idea.

"What if I practiced lots and trained Theodore even more before the wedding?" I asked. "I'll make sure everything is *perfect*. I promise!"

Dad sighed. "I don't think that's a good idea, Mindy. The wedding is in two days, and Theodore—"

Before Dad could continue, Julie grabbed his arm. She gave him a little smile, and he slowly nodded.

Julie turned back to me and said, "I know how important Theodore is to you, Mindy. We both do. We'll give you one more chance. Just make sure to bring his leash on Sunday, okay? In case things don't work out."

I squeezed Julie tight and jumped up and down.

"Thanks, Julie! I promise you won't regret it!"

I was determined to do my very best for the big day!

Chapter 5

After the rehearsal dinner, Dad talked to one of the workers. He sounded super worried, so when he was done, I asked him what was wrong.

"Apparently, the forecast for this weekend is rain," Dad said. "Luckily, the hotel is willing to move the wedding indoors if it really does rain. But it still changes a lot of things, so this is all very stressful!"

"Oh no!" I felt bad for Dad and Julie. They'd worked so hard to plan the perfect wedding. And I remembered how happy they were about the view. It would really stink if everything got ruined!

When we got back home, Dad talked on the

phone with Julie for a long time. He sounded so disappointed. I felt sad just listening to him.

I wanted to help them have the best wedding ever, but I couldn't control the weather. I could help with the other stuff, though! Like practicing for the wedding. And training Theodore!

I borrowed Keun Appa's laptop and video-called Sally.

When she picked up, Sally asked, "Hi, Mindy! How was the practice? Are you excited for the big day?"

"Yeah!" I replied. "But I'm also a little worried."

"Aw, how come?"

I told Sally about what happened at the rehearsal, and how both Theodore and I made a big scene in front of everybody.

"It's okay, Mindy! A lot always happens at weddings. If something goes wrong, it's normal! I've been to a few, so I know what they're like."

"But I want Julie and Dad to have a perfect,

fairy-tale wedding!" I said. "Like your cousin's in Hawaii."

Sally giggled. "That wedding was super pretty, but a lot of things still went wrong. A bird pooped on my cousin's head. And someone knocked over the cake! But in the end, none of that mattered, because you could tell everyone loved each other very much. That's the most important thing! We're celebrating your dad and Julie. And they both love you, and each other, no matter what happens!"

Sally was right. What mattered the most was that we would all be together and have a good time!

"Thanks for the good advice, Sally! I still want to do my best to help Dad and Julie, though. So I better get busy tomorrow."

"You're welcome. We're not really doing anything this weekend besides the wedding on Sunday. If you need any help, I can come over!"

"That'd be awesome. Thanks, Sally!"

I really have the greatest best friend!

That night, Grandpa told my cousins and me a bedtime story. I was excited to hear a story with my cousins. Since I live in America and they live in Korea, I almost never get a chance to listen to Grandpa's stories!

"Min-jung, your dad told me you have a book

of Korean folk tales, but have you heard the story about why frogs cry when it rains?"

My book has a story about the frogs, but I lied and said it didn't. I wanted to hear Grandpa's version of the story!

Grandpa sat us down in the living room, campfire-style, and told us the story of the naughty frog who didn't listen to his mom. He would do the opposite of everything his mom told him to—until it was too late. Before the mom died, she thought the frog would continue doing the opposite of what she said, so she asked to be buried on low ground instead of high ground. But the sad frog wanted to be a good kid and followed her directions, and when it rained, the water swept the mom's grave away!

"So that's why frogs cry every time it rains. It's because they miss their moms! And all of this is an important lesson to listen to your parents before it's too late!"

I gulped. Even though I already knew how the story ended, it hit too close to home today!

Before Julie stepped in, Dad didn't want Theodore to come to the wedding. What if things went terribly wrong at the wedding, all because I didn't listen to him?

I said good night to everyone and then crawled into my own bed. Before I went to sleep, I closed my eyes and made a quick wish.

I really hoped that Theodore and I wouldn't ruin Dad and Julie's wedding day!

Chapter 6

The next day, I was determined to make sure every-thing went smoothly at Dad's wedding tomorrow. Even though I knew it didn't have to be perfect, I still wanted to make it as good as I could.

Dad and my grandparents were busy with preparations for the wedding, so Keun Appa and Keun Umma were at the house with us. I told them about my plans to make Dad's wedding the best wedding ever. And I had some *big* plans.

We only had one day left, so I could use all the help I could get!

"Aw, that's so sweet of you, Min-jung!" Keun

Umma said. "Let's go get your friend Sally!"

After we picked up Sally, my aunt and uncle took my cousins, Sally, and me to the nearest party store. There we found fake flower petals for me, and a dog ring-bearer tuxedo outfit for Theodore. It was a whole-family effort!

The first thing we had to do when we got back home was make sure I wouldn't trip during the real ceremony.

"Okay," Sally said. "I was a flower girl at my cousin's wedding, and it was pretty easy, but the trick is to not get distracted by people in the audience. You have to watch where you're going!"

With my basket filled with fake flower petals, I practiced walking up and down the living room a few times. Sally and my relatives sat in rows in the living room, pretending there was an aisle in the middle of the space. They all stared at me and cheered, just like they would at the actual wedding.

I was nervous at first, but by the third or fourth

time, I felt much better! Sally was right. Keeping my eyes on where I was going helped!

Next, Keun Umma helped me put the ring-bearer outfit on Theodore. It looked like a tiny suit, and with his beard, Theodore looked like a cute little old man!

The outfit had a harness with a pillow on his back for the wed- ding rings. We couldn't use the real rings for

practice, so I used two plastic flower rings I'd got- ten from cupcakes my friends brought for their birthdays in class.

Theodore looked so handsome and cute with his dog tuxedo and rings!

But even though I thought he was cute, Theodore didn't seem so sure. He twisted around and rolled on the floor, trying to take off his harness!

"No, Theodore!" I said. "This is your big moment!"

It was like Theodore had forgotten every-thing he'd learned from when I'd trained him with Eunice. First he got really distracted by everyone and wanted pats and cuddles. Then he decided it was a good time to lie down and take a nap.

Luckily, I had my relatives and Sally to help. We grabbed a few of Theodore's favorite treats and worked together to train my dog.

It took us a while, but when we were done, Theodore could walk up and down in a straight line by himself with the ring-bearer outfit on. I hoped he would do this tomorrow, too!

The last thing on our to-do list for the day was to make some small gifts for Julie. We were trying our best to incorporate both Chinese *and* Korean culture into the wedding for Julie and her family!

With Keun Appa's help, we looked up lucky Chinese wedding traditions on the computer.

"Okay, Mindy," said Keun Appa. "This website says that the guests at the wedding should give the bride and groom money in red envelopes so they'll have good luck. Keun Umma and I already bought red envelopes so all the adults can give them money. But do you have any ideas on what you and the other kids can do?"

I thought for a second. Sally, my cousins, and I didn't have money . . . what could we give instead?

And then I got an idea.

"I know! We can draw our own money with happy pictures! That'd be super lucky for sure!"

"Great idea! I'm sure your dad and Julie will love that."

So the other kids and I sat around the kitchen table and drew our own dollar bills with pictures of Julie, Dad, Theodore, and me as one big happy family. We also drew lucky Chinese symbols we found online, like the double-happiness symbol, dragons, and phoenixes!

Sora is still really little, so her people looked
more like big snowmen. And Theodore looked
like a bear! But she drew big smiles on everyone's
faces, and her drawings were so cute, so I didn't
say anything.

"Hey, Mindy," Sally said while we were draw-
ing. "So, tomorrow's the big day! Julie's going to
be a part of your forever family soon. How are you
feeling?"

I bit my lip. I'd been so busy preparing for the

ceremony that I hadn't really thought about how much of a big change tomorrow was going to bring.

But then I thought back to the happy memories Dad, Julie, and I had shared together, like celebrating Lunar New Year, going to the fall carnival, and winning the school trivia competition.

"Julie's been part of Dad's and my family for a long time," I said. "This wedding is a big deal, but it's just one more memory we're going to share together. And hopefully we'll have a lot more after that!"

Sally gave me a big grin. "Yeah! I'm sure you guys will."

Soon we had a bunch of paper drawings stuffed in the red envelopes.

By the end of the day, we were ready for the wedding!

Chapter 7

Tomorrow morning was going to be busy with the different wedding activities, so we dropped Theodore the Mutt off at Sally's house when we gave her a ride back home.

"I'll make sure to bring him right in time for the wedding ceremony!" said Sally as she got out of the car. "Along with everyone in my family, of course."

We laughed.

"Thanks, Sally!" I said. "See you tomorrow!"

"See you! Good luck!"

When we arrived back home, Dad tucked me

in bed. After the busy day, this quiet moment alone with him was nice.

"Tomorrow's going to be hectic, so I just want to make sure—you're still okay with staying at Eunice's house while Julie and I are on our honeymoon, right?" Dad asked.

"Yup!" I said. "Don't worry about me, and have a great time with Julie!"

"Thanks, Mindy. You have fun with Theodore and Oliver, okay?"

Oliver the Maltese is Eunice's dog. He's cute, and he's Theodore's best friend! I love seeing the two of them play together.

"You got it! I'll send you and Julie lots of cute dog pictures."

"Whew, thank goodness," Dad said. "I didn't know what I'd do without the cuteness. I'm sure Julie feels the same way!"

I giggled and Dad gave me another hug.

"How are you feeling, by the way?" Dad asked. "About everything? Sorry I got mad at you during the wedding rehearsal, Mindy. I was just caught off guard by what happened with Theodore, and I felt bad and ashamed because I didn't want our dog to ruin the wedding. It may be my second time getting married, but that's not the case for Julie."

I looked down at my hands. "It's okay, Appa. I understand. I felt bad about what happened during the rehearsal too. I should have told you about my plans for Theodore."

"That's all right, Mindy. We live and we learn. Were you and Theodore able to practice some more for the big day?"

"Yup! We worked really hard. I can't wait for you and Julie to see Theodore in his ring-bearer outfit!"

Dad chuckled. "I'm excited to see it! And I'm excited to see *you* as the flower girl as well. You're both going to do great."

He patted my head, and I beamed.

"How are *you* feeling, Appa?" I asked. "Tomorrow's the big day!"

Dad nervously smiled. "I'm excited! But also scared. I hope all the preparations will be worth it!"

"Don't worry. We've all been working hard to make tomorrow good! I'll make sure the wedding's going to be great!"

"Thanks, Mindy. I appreciate how hard you and everyone else worked to prepare for everything, but I also want you to know that it's all right if things aren't perfect, okay? Sorry, did my stressing out about the wedding make you worried?"

I shook my head. "No, that's not it."

I bit my lip. I'd never really thought about why I wanted the wedding to be so perfect, but now, as I was talking to Dad, I sort of figured out why.

I looked at the framed picture of Mom, Dad, and me on my bedside table.

"I want this wedding to be perfect so that you and Julie can have a happily ever after! If I tripped again or if something else went wrong in the wedding, I'd feel really bad. I don't want to jinx things for you and Julie!"

Dad's eyes became shiny, and he pulled me into a big hug. When he let go of me, he reached over to grab the picture I was staring at.

"Mindy," he said, his voice sounding all choked and funny. "In a way, your mom and I did have our own happily ever after. Don't get me wrong—I really wish we hadn't lost her like we did. She left us so soon. But she and I made amazing memories together. And we had you! She's gone now, but you're still here. And you're the best daughter I could ever ask for. So, *you're* our happily ever after, okay?"

When he was done talking, I was crying too. "You're my happily ever after too. And I'm really excited Julie is going to be a part of that now."

He put the picture down on my bedside table and pulled me in for another hug. "Life doesn't

have to be perfect, Mindy. Sure, trying our best is important, but at the end of the day, it's the good memories we have together that count. Because those last forever."

"Okay. Then I hope we make lots of good memories tomorrow!"

"I'm sure we will. Julie and I are so lucky to have you. Thank you."

"You're welcome, Appa. I'm lucky to have you and Julie, too!"

We let go of each other, and Dad said, "Good night, Mindy. Sleep tight!"

"You too, Appa!" I replied. "Let's have a good wedding tomorrow!"

Chapter 8

When I woke up the morning of the wedding, it was really quiet. Normally when it rained, I could hear the splish-splash of water. But not today.

"It's not raining!" I yelled. It was so sunny outside! It was a wedding-day miracle.

I raced downstairs and hugged everyone, spending an extra-long time in Dad's arms. He squeezed me tight and smiled. We were all so happy!

"The rain must have come and gone while we were sleeping," Dad said. "What a perfect start to today!"

We all got dressed for the wedding. Grandma changed into her hanbok while Dad, Grandpa, and Keun Appa got into their tuxedos. My cousins and I wore nice clothes that the adults had bought us for the wedding. I was wearing a pretty pink dress that Julie got me!

Finally, Dad and I packed our hanbok so we could wear them for the Korean ceremony later today.

When we finished getting ready, Mr. Johnson—Sally's dad—and a few of Dad's other guy friends showed up at our door. Along with Keun Appa and me, they were Dad's side of the wedding party!

As part of Chinese tradition, we were all going to pick up Julie for the wedding. This was just one of the many ways we were incorporating Julie's culture along with ours for the festivities!

Dad drove Keun Appa and me to Julie's house, while the other groomsmen followed behind us in their cars. As we approached Julie's street, the drivers started honking. It was like a parade!

"In Chinese culture, people play door games on the morning of the wedding!" Dad explained while we were in the car. "The groom has to pass a few tests by the bride's family and friends to prove himself worthy of the bride."

"Games?" I said. "That sounds like fun! Can I play too?"

"Of course, Mindy! The groomsmen can help the groom when they have to, like they're all part of the same team. And you're the most important member!"

At Julie's, six of her friends stood in front of her house, guarding the door. The ladies were all dressed in beautiful matching dresses. They were her bridesmaids! Sally's mom and Keun Umma were there too.

"Brian Kim!" Mrs. Johnson said to Dad. "You can't pass and see your bride until you've done our challenges! The first door-game challenge is to answer questions about Julie. If you get a question wrong, you'll have to do push-ups!"

Dad looked nervous, but the groomsmen and I gave him encouraging smiles.

"You can do it, Appa!" I cheered him on.

"Okay," he said. "Let's do this!"

"What is Julie's favorite color?" asked Brianna, Julie's best friend.

"Blue!" Dad said. "That's an easy one."

"What's her favorite food?" asked Keun Umma.

I bit my lip. I knew this one! But I wanted to give Dad a chance to answer, so I kept quiet.

"Steamed buns!" Dad said. "Especially the ones with barbecue pork in them."

"Correct!" said one of Julie's other friends. "Okay, last question. What is Julie's favorite memory from childhood?"

Dad blinked. "I don't think she ever told me this one. But she did say that she loved traveling around the United States with her parents!"

"That's also correct! Congrats, you got all of them right!"

We all cheered. We were one step closer to seeing Julie!

Dad and his team had to do two other challenges. One included having to give Julie's friends red envelopes full of money that were in multiples of lucky Chinese numbers like eight and nine. I didn't have money, so I gave them one of the red envelopes with my drawings in it!

My favorite door-game activity was called Pass the Seaweed, in which we had to pass pieces of seaweed around with our mouths! It was fun watching Dad and the other grown-ups on our team play. Dad always passed the seaweed to me. Since I was at the end of the line, I felt like an important part of the team! All that seaweed reminded me of the yummy seaweed business I started in school when we first moved to Florida.

Everyone was laughing by the end of the game. We managed to pass all the pieces of seaweed without dropping a single one!

And then, finally, it was time to see Julie!

Julie's friends blindfolded Dad and walked him into the house while he talked about all the reasons why he loved Julie. It was funny and sweet to watch, especially when he had to pick out shoes for Julie while blindfolded!

At first Dad held up a flip-flop, and then a boot. Everyone laughed until Dad picked a nice pair of flats for Julie to wear at the wedding.

We all helped Dad through the house, until we reached the living room.

Julie was waiting for us on the couch. She was dressed in a pretty *qipao*, a traditional red Chinese dress with gold embroidery. She looked so beautiful!

Julie's bridesmaids undid Dad's blindfold so he could finally see Julie.

He put the shoes on Julie's feet and then gave her a big hug.

They both looked so happy!

Chapter 9

After lunch at Julie's house, we went to the hotel. There was still a lot of time before the wedding ceremony with all the other guests, but my relatives and I were going early for the Chinese tea ceremony!

The tearoom was decorated with red lanterns, flowers, and red and gold cushions. There was also a big gold Chinese symbol on the wall. It was the double-happiness symbol I'd found online while we were making the paper money!

Since Julie and Dad are both the youngest in their families, they had to serve tea to their siblings

as well as their parents. I watched with my cousins as the adults participated in the ceremony.

Everyone had really nice things to say, but my favorite moment was when Julie said to her parents, "Thank you so much for everything. I know raising me in America wasn't easy, but you two are the best parents I could have ever asked for."

When it was his turn, Dad thanked his parents too. By the end, there was not a dry eye in the room!

Dad's and Julie's families gave them gifts, including red envelopes and gold jewelry. When all the grown-ups were done, my cousins and I gave Julie and Dad the rest of our red envelopes.

"Oh my gosh, these are so cute!" Julie said. "Thank you, everyone!"

"What a sweet gesture!" said Julie's mom.

"It was Min-jung's idea!" Sung-jin said. "She wanted to do something special for Julie."

"We don't have money, so we filled the red

envelopes with drawings instead," I explained. "Sally helped too!"

"Great job, all of you," Dad said as he smiled proudly at my cousins and me.

I grinned. I was so happy that everyone liked our red envelopes!

Chapter 10

When it was finally time for the American wedding ceremony, I was super nervous. My family, Sally, and I had worked so hard to prepare for this special day! I really hoped everything would go well.

While we all waited for Julie to change out of her *qipao* and into her white wedding dress, I met up with Sally and Theodore in the outdoor deck area and said hi to Eunice, her parents, and the other guests seated in the chairs. A lot of them said "ooh" and "aah" because of how pretty the ocean view was. A small orchestra got their instruments ready, and even though they were just practicing, I could tell they were going to sound great!

I was really glad it didn't rain after all!

Even though everything looked pretty, seeing so many people outside made me feel kind of queasy. I tried my best to ignore them by talking to Sally.

"Thanks again for helping out," I said. "I couldn't do any of this without you!"

"No problem," Sally replied. "I love weddings, and you're my best friend, so I'm happy to help out!"

The plan was for Sally to stay with Theodore while I walked down the aisle. Hopefully, that would prevent him from running off like he did at the practice!

The orchestra started playing a loud, happy song. I gulped. It was time to go down the aisle!

Sally gave me a quick hug before I ran back inside.

Julie's mom came out and walked down the aisle first, then Dad, Keun Appa, and Julie's and

Dad's friends. I waited with Theodore until it was my turn to go.

Before I went down the aisle, I made sure to tell Theodore to stay. He sat on his butt and waited. Sally gave me a thumbs-up. So far so good!

I clutched my flower basket tightly as I walked. Everyone was watching me, smiling and taking pictures as I went past them and sprinkled the flowers. My legs shook just a tiny bit and my face hurt from the big grin I had on my face. But like I'd practiced, I kept my attention on my feet. This time, I didn't trip!

And then it was Theodore's turn. I put my basket down and took a deep breath. This was the big moment of truth!

"Come here, boy!" I said.

Sally unhooked Theodore from his leash.

The crowd laughed and said "Aww!" as he ran down the aisle in his ring-bearer outfit. He looked so handsome! I hoped everyone was getting lots of

65

cute pictures of him so I could see them later!

When Theodore reached me at the front, I gave him a treat.

"Good boy!" I exclaimed while petting him. "You're the best boy ever!"

"Great job training him, Mindy!" Dad whispered. "You, Sally, and Theodore did an amazing job!"

I smiled at Sally, and she grinned back. I felt really proud of the three of us. We did it!

Theodore wagged his tail. He looked so happy and proud of us too.

And then it was finally time for Julie and her dad to walk down the aisle.

When Julie came out in her sparkling white wedding dress, my jaw almost dropped to the floor. She was so pretty, like a Disney princess!

Dad looked amazed too. His mouth hung open, like he couldn't believe how lucky he was.

During the ceremony, Dad and Julie said they felt so grateful they were able to find each other.

Everyone started crying during their vows, and there were sniffles all around.

At the end of the ceremony, Dad and Julie pulled me in for a hug. Everyone clapped and cheered! Theodore joined in with a little bark and lots of tail wagging.

Even though I would never forget Mom, I was glad that Julie was now an official part of our family. We all made one another so happy! And I knew Mom would be happy for us too.

Chapter 11

I was so relieved that the American ceremony was over. My job was mostly done!

But we weren't finished yet. Now it was time for more festivities!

Julie, Dad, and I went to go change into our hanbok. Keun Umma helped me get into the yellow-and-red hanbok I got during our trip to Korea. Dad and Julie were still getting ready by the time I was done, so I went into the reception hall first.

"Min-jung, you look so beautiful!" said Grandpa when he saw me in my hanbok.

I beamed. "Thanks, Harabeoji!"

He and Grandma looked so proud and happy to see me in my traditional Korean clothes. Even though I'd gotten fitted for everything during our trip, this was the first time my family from Korea was seeing me in the hanbok. My relatives and I took a lot of pictures while waiting for Julie and Dad to come out.

A few minutes later, Julie and Dad entered the hall, followed by two Chinese lions—one gold and one white. Dad looked so handsome in his traditional blue hanbok for grooms, while Julie looked like a princess in her red hanbok for brides. They looked like they'd come out of a Korean fairy tale!

People with gongs and drums followed close behind, playing a medley of Korean and Chinese songs. Everyone was bobbing their heads to the beat and having a good time. It was really cool how Dad and Julie managed to mix both Chinese and Korean traditions into the celebration!

The lions got onto the stage and danced, doing

tricks that made people laugh and go, "Wow!" Lots of guests had their phones out, taking pictures and videos, too.

Sally, my cousins, and I got closer to the stage so we could get a better view.

"This reminds me of the Chinese lions we saw at the Lunar New Year parade!" Sally exclaimed.

"Same here!" I said.

Thinking of the Lunar New Year parade made me smile. That was the first time I'd met Julie, who was then just one of Dad's friends from work. So much had changed since then!

Dad and Julie sat on the stage while the two lions danced together in front of them. The dance ended with the lions coming together for a big kiss. Everyone said "aww" and cheered! It was such a fun and sweet performance!

When the lions left, my grandparents and I got onto the stage. It was now time for *paebaek*, the Korean wedding ceremony!

People came up onto the stage with us to help set up chairs, a small table, and other traditional Korean decorations. The food towers, sweets platters, and Korean tea set looked so pretty. When everything was set up, my grandparents and I sat in the chairs in front of Julie and Dad.

An emcee named Ms. Jang came out with a microphone to help explain to the crowd what was happening, in English and Korean.

"First, as part of the Korean ceremony, we will have the bride and groom pay respects to the groom's family," she said. "Traditionally, the parents are supposed to drink a shot of rice wine to show that they approve of the bride. But we will just be using water today, since the wonderful Mindy will be participating with her grandparents!"

Everyone smiled, and I did too. I was really glad I was a part of this ceremony!

Ms. Jang poured water into our small cups.

When it was time to ask for approval, Julie and

Dad bowed down to my grandparents and me.

"Of course we accept you, Julie!" I exclaimed.

I swallowed the water in one big gulp. My grandparents drank the water too.

Everyone laughed and cheered. Julie officially had our family's approval!

Afterward, my grandparents and I stepped to the side so Julie's parents could do the same thing for Dad. I cheered as her parents drank the water. He had their approval too!

The next part of the Korean ceremony was a game where my grandparents and Julie's parents had to throw chestnuts and dates to see how many children Dad and Julie were going to have.

My grandparents tossed them and got six!

Next, Julie's parents did the same thing. Four!

Julie and Dad shared a smile, and everyone giggled.

I'd always wanted siblings, but I wasn't sure how I felt about having ten of them!

Afterward, Ms. Jang said, "Okay, now we're going to play another game to see what gender the first baby will be. Brian, do you want a boy or a girl?"

Dad thought hard about it and then said, "Girl! It'd be nice if Mindy could have a sister."

"How about you, Julie?" Ms. Jang asked.

"Boy!" Julie said. "I come from a family of three girls, and although I love my sisters, we have enough girls in our family."

Everyone laughed.

Ms. Jang walked Dad and Julie through the next steps. They had to take a date in their mouths and bite into it together to see which person got the pit.

Dad and Julie put the date between their mouths and pulled. It was like they were kissing, but funnier and cuter!

"I got the pit!" Julie finally said.

We all laughed and cheered.

I guess that meant I was going to have a baby brother!

Last but not least, Dad had to carry Julie around piggyback to show that he could support her and the rest of our family. He and Julie both had wide grins on their faces as they went around the stage, and we were all smiling too.

Everyone was so happy! It really was the perfect fairy-tale wedding.

Chapter 12

After all the ceremonies were over, Dad and Julie had their first dance while Keun Appa sang for them and played guitar. It was so romantic!

Sally sighed happily as we watched them dance.

"See?" she said. "I told you your dad and Julie were meant to be. It's just like in the movies."

I laughed. "Yeah, you were right. Thanks for being their number-one fan from the very beginning!"

When it was our time to hit the dance floor, I twirled around with Sally. My cousins joined in,

After all the ceremonies were over, Dad and Julie had their first dance while Keun Appa sang for them and played guitar. It was so romantic!

Sally sighed happily as we watched them dance.

"See?" she said. "I told you your dad and Julie were meant to be. It's just like in the movies."

I laughed. "Yeah, you were right. Thanks for being their number-one fan from the very beginning!"

When it was our time to hit the dance floor, I twirled around with Sally. My cousins joined in,

and so did Sally's sisters. We jumped up and down to the music. It was a really fun time!

At the end of the night, everyone stood outside the hotel with sparklers as Dad and Julie ran to the car. Sally was right. This wedding really was like a scene out of a movie!

When he spotted me, Dad swept me up into a big hug.

"You did it, Appa!" I said. "And you too, Julie! You guys are married now!"

Julie smiled and joined our hug. "We did! Thanks, Mindy. We couldn't have done it without you!"

"Yes," Dad said. "You did so much for us, Mindy! I'm always so, so grateful to be your dad. But now all the hard stuff is over, so have fun with Eunice, Theodore, and Oliver while Julie and I are gone, okay? Don't be afraid to call if you need anything!"

I squeezed Julie and Dad tight.

"I'm going to miss you two so much. But have

lots of fun in Key West! Say hi to the manatees and dolphins for me if you ever see them!"

"Definitely. We'll send you pictures, too!"

Dad and Julie got in the car, and I waved until I couldn't see them anymore.

"Mindy, are you okay?" Sally asked. "You're crying!"

I blinked and rubbed my eyes. Sally was right. My eyes had teared up while I was watching Dad and Julie leave!

"Yeah," I said. "I'm not crying because I'm sad. I'm crying because I'm happy."

"That's good," Sally said. "Want to go back inside and get ice cream before we leave?"

"Yeah!"

"I want ice cream too!" Sora said.

"Me too!" said Sung-jin.

"Let's all race to get ice cream!" Sally said. "On your mark, get set, go!"

We all ran back inside, giggling and screaming.

It was a whole new adventure for Dad and Julie, but it'd also be a whole new adventure for them and me—as one big happy family—when they got back!

Acknowledgments

I still remember the first time I saw my parents' wedding video (back when it was on VCR!) as well as the second time I watched it a few years later (after we had it converted to DVD, haha). Disney paints the picture of a perfect fairy-tale wedding, but my parents' ceremony is what I always imagine when I think of mine. Because of this and much more, I'd first like to thank my parents, whose patience, resilience, and love are the backbone of our family.

My family is not bicultural (other than being Korean American), but I was inspired by the many

Korean and Chinese (as well as other interracial) American couples' wedding videos I watched on YouTube as I wrote this book. I'll refrain from mentioning specific names here so as to respect their privacy, but I wish all the couples health, happiness, and love. Thank you for sharing such a beautiful moment from your lives.

Most of the Mindy Kim books came out (and are coming out) during the COVID-19 pandemic, which means that most of my time as a published author has been spent in relative isolation. As a result, the emails, letters, and other correspondence I receive from readers, parents, librarians, booksellers, and educators mean the world to me. Thank you so much for all your support! And of course, thank you as always to my agent, Penny Moore; my illustrator, Dung Ho; my editor, Alyson Heller; and the rest of my team at Simon & Schuster for making these books possible. Here's to the third year of Mindy books!

On a personal level, I'd also like to thank my friends, especially those who continue to support Mindy to this very day. Brianna Lei, Bernice Yau, Stephanie Lu, Alisha Erin Hillam, Priyanka Taslim, Rachel Simon, Alice Zhu, Annie Lee, June Hur, Sheila Holsinger, and so many others I am so lucky to call my friends, thank you so much for everything.

Finally, thank you to my partner, Sean Dillard, who is heating up cookies for me as I finish up these revisions on a holiday weekend. Thank you for all your love and support for me and our fur baby, Eiva the Siberian Husky. Being new dog parents isn't easy (especially when deadlines are involved), but we're making it work! I'm so excited to have our own fairy-tale wedding someday.

About the Author

Lyla Lee is the author of the Mindy Kim series as well as the upcoming *Flip the Script* for teens. Born in South Korea, she's since then lived in various parts of the United States, including California, Florida, and Texas. Inspired by her English teacher, she started writing her own stories in fourth grade and finished her first novel at the age of fourteen. After working in Hollywood and studying psychology and cinematic arts at the University of Southern California, she now lives in Dallas, Texas. When she is not writing, she is teaching kids or playing with her dog, Eiva the Siberian husky. You can visit her online at lylaleebooks.com.